L is for
LOVE

To Angela, Lizzie and Jules, who labour in love with me ♥ **A**

For Beth and Jack, all you need is Love x ♥ **A.B.**

WALKER BOOKS
AND SUBSIDIARIES
LONDON · BOSTON · SYDNEY · AUCKLAND

First published 2024 by Walker Books Ltd, 87 Vauxhall Walk, London SE11 5HJ · Text © 2024 Atinuke ♥ Illustrations © 2024 Angela Brooksbank ♥ The right of Atinuke and Angela Brooksbank to be identified as author and illustrator respectively of this work has been asserted in accordance with the Copyright, Designs and Patents Act 1988 ♥ This book has been typeset in Shinn ♥ Printed in China ♥ All rights reserved. No part of this book may be reproduced, transmitted or stored in an information retrieval system in any form or by any means, graphic, electronic or mechanical, including photocopying, taping and recording, without prior written permission from the publisher ♥ British Library Cataloguing in Publication Data: a catalogue record for this book is available from the British Library
ISBN 978-1-5295-0148-3 ♥ www.walker.co.uk ♥ 10 9 8 7 6 5 4 3 2 1

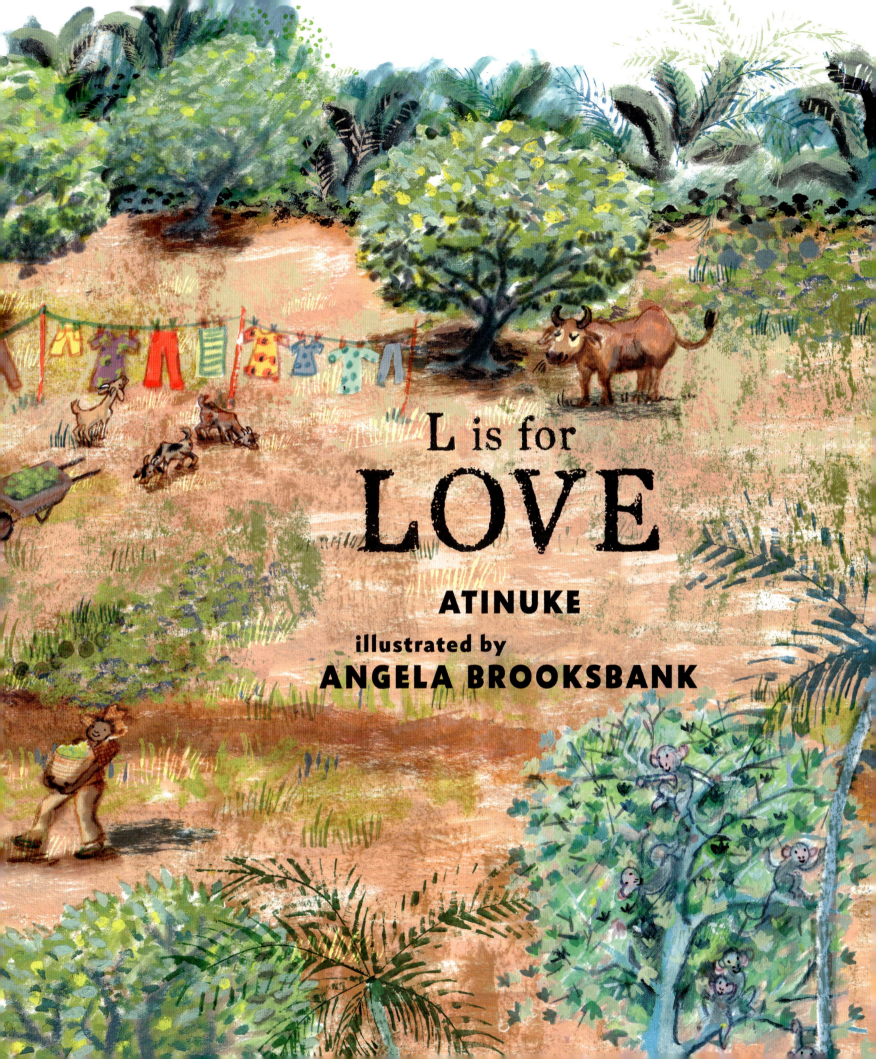

L is for
LOVE

ATINUKE

illustrated by
ANGELA BROOKSBANK

L is for
Love
and
L is for
Lemons.

L is for **Leaving**,
L is for **Linger**,

L is for
Lamp.

L is for **Loads.**

L is for **Legs.**

L is for **Log.**

L is for **Limp.**

L is for **Lorry.**

L is for **Lift.**

L is for **Lucky.**

L is for **Lightning,**

and L is for ...

Light!

Look!
L is for
Lazy Lions.

Look!
L is for
Lonely Leopard.

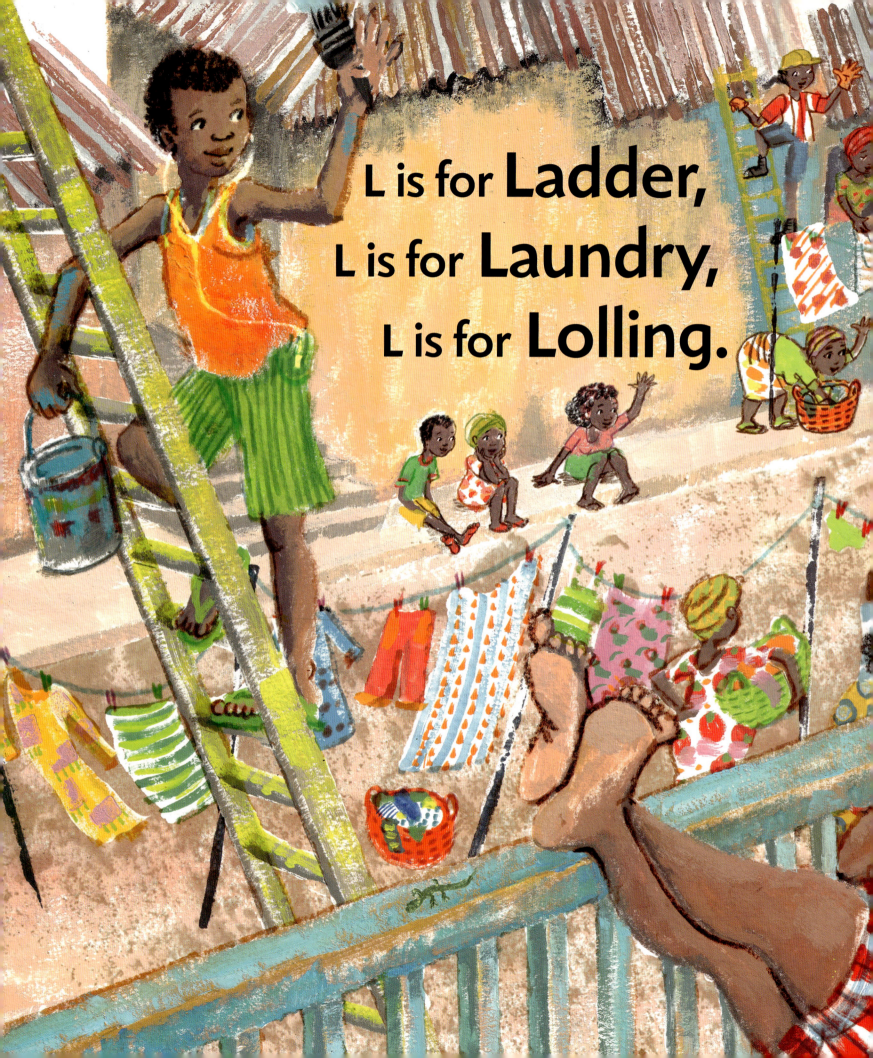

L is for **Ladder**,
L is for **Laundry**,
L is for **Lolling**.

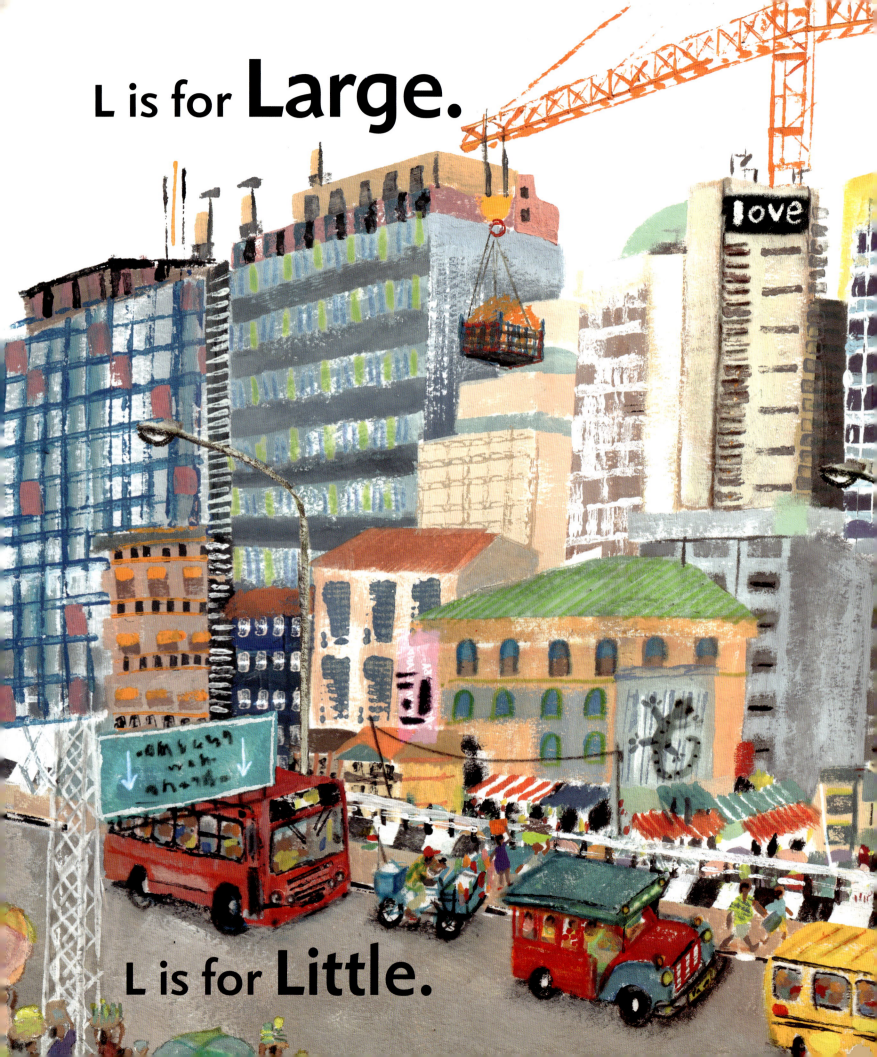

L is for **Large.**

L is for **Little.**

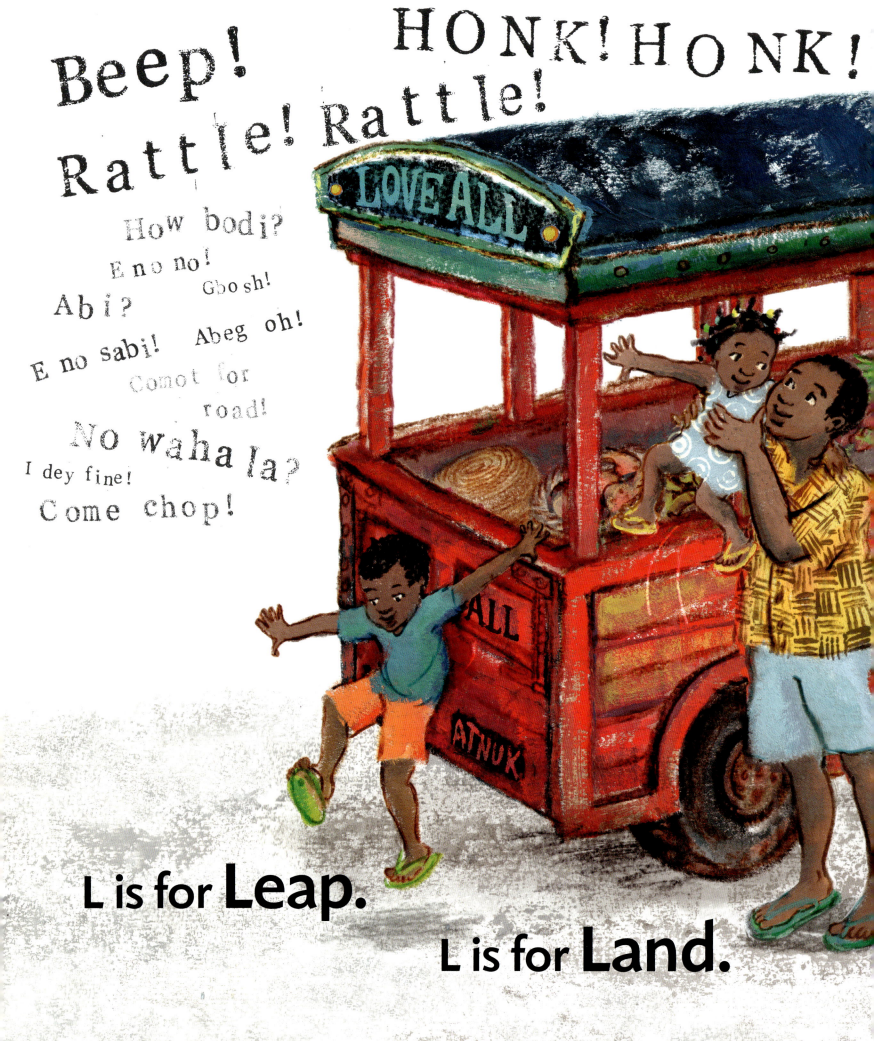

Beep! HONK! HONK!
Rattle! Rattle!

How bodi?
E no no!
Abi? Gbosh!
E no sabi! Abeg oh!
Comot for road!
No wahala?
I dey fine!
Come chop!

LOVE ALL

L is for **Leap.**

L is for **Land.**

HONK! Rattle! Beep! Beep!

Honk!

E too cost!

Rattle! Rattle!

Bang! Bang!

Le's go! Na so?

Oya na!

GBAM?!

L is for **Listen.**

L is for **Loud.**

L is for
LAGOS!

L is for **Lace.**
L is for **Lovely.**

L is for
Lemons.

L is for
Lids.

L is for
Leaf.

L is for
Lunch.

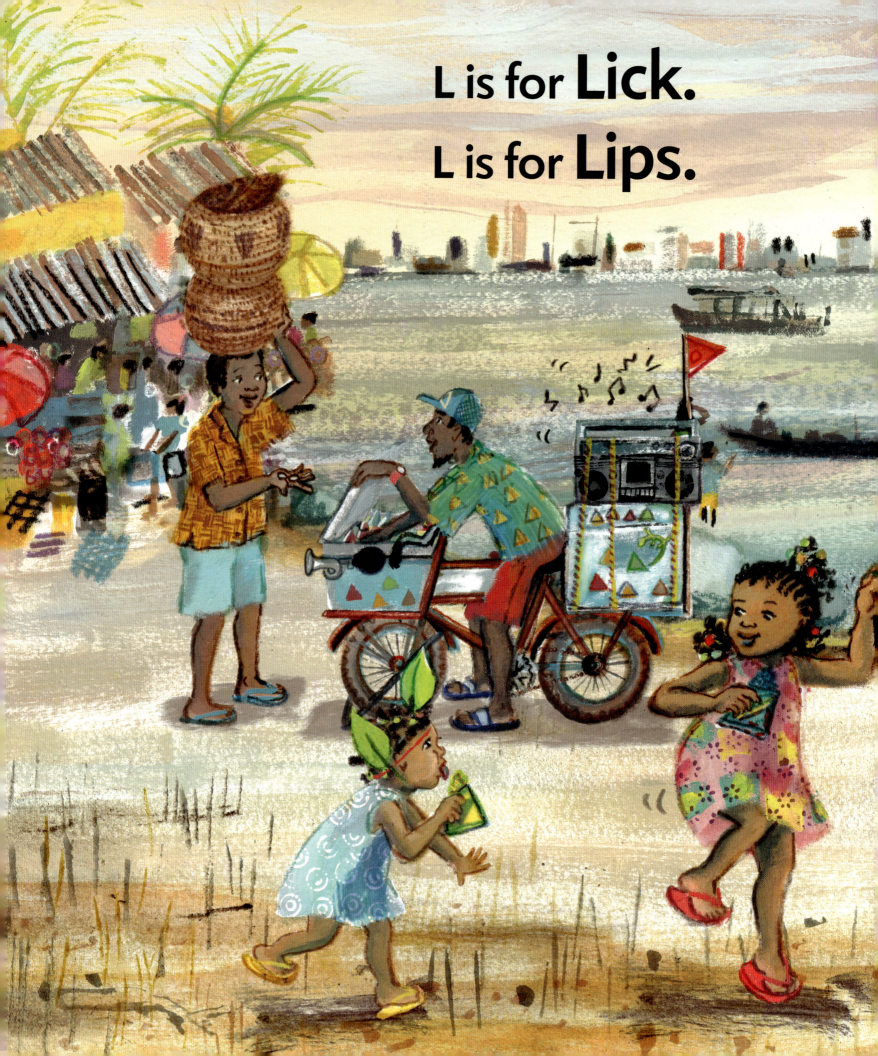

L is for **Lick.**
L is for **Lips.**

L is for **Laugh.**

L is for **Long way home.**

L is for **Late**,

and L is for ...

Love!